# Can YOU make a SCARY FACE?

by jan thomas

**beach lane books**

new york  london  toronto  sydney

HA!

Hmm . . . It TICKLES?

WIGGLE YOUR NOSE and LAUGH!

Wait.
The tiny TICKLY bug is
out of your mouth, but
NOW it's in your SHIRT?

The only way to GET IT OUT is to...

DO THE CHICKEN DANCE!

Don't worry. **PRETEND** there's a giant hungry frog coming to eat that tiny **TICKLY** bug **STUCK** in your shirt!

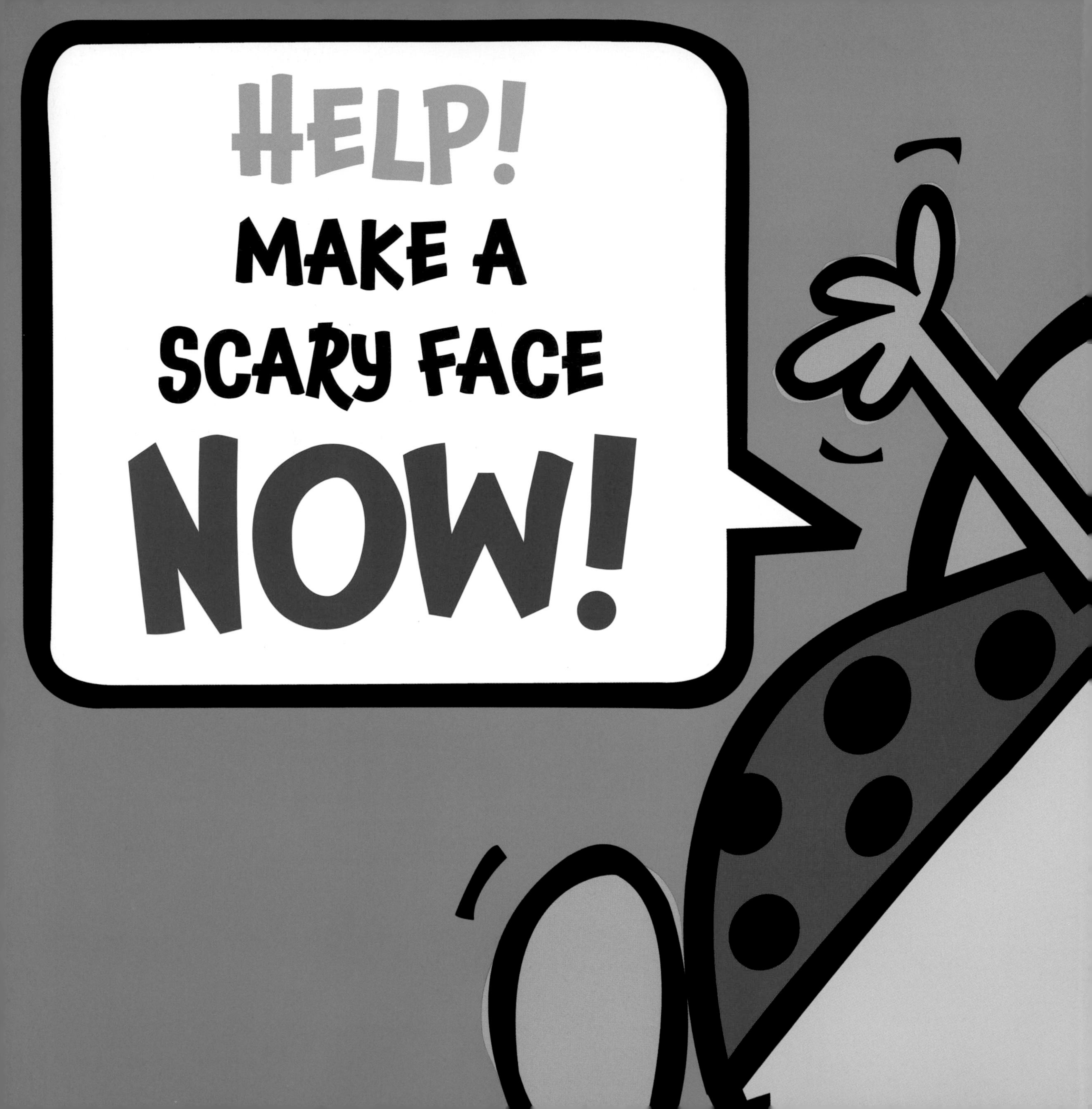
HELP!
MAKE A
SCARY FACE
NOW!